There was once a kingdom far away –

Not too sunny, not too gray,

Not too big and not too small –

Just a kingdom – that's all.

And the kingdom was ruled by a king –

Not too big and not too small,

Not too short and not too tall,

Not too foolish, not too bright –

Just a man – just right.

And the king had a daughter, a princess –

And the princess, so I'm told,

Was not too fat and not too scrawny,

Not too pale and not too brawny,

Not too sweet and not too tart –

But, my goodness, she was smart!

Even as a child,

She had questions to ask

and answers to seek;

Her list of inquiries grew

longer each week –

And the king's wise counselors

were all overwrought,

Just from trying to find her

the answers she sought.

And the years went by,

as years tend to do,

And alone in the castle

the princess grew.

With the years,

she grew older...

and taller... and sadder...

For she didn't have friends

to make her heart gladder.

She had all that she wanted

to nurture her mind,

But she needed a friend

who was helpful and kind!

And the king thought,

"Now where, in this kingdom so fair,

Is a friend for my daughter,

a friend who will care?"

He assembled his sages, his counselors all,

And sat them at desks in the Great Royal Hall,

And he said, "You must work now, by day and by night;

Your most clever ideas I command you to write –

Just how we will find my dear daughter a friend

To delight her sad heart and her sorrows to end."

He provided the sages with fine food and drink,

And huge piles of paper and barrels of ink,

And they covered those papers with millions of signs,

With formulas, diagrams, sketches of lines,

And a chart of the distance from Earth to the Sun –

But not one successful proposal. Not even one.

"Your Majesty," said they, despairing at length,

"Your question has worn out our minds and our strength!

If three hundred sages can't do what you ask,

We must ask the princess for help with our task!

We're sure she'll come up with a brilliant suggestion

On just how, exactly, to answer your question."

So the king sent his messenger swiftly to call

The princess to come to the Great Royal Hall –

Where the counselors sat in their gowns and their caps

With test tubes and telescopes, notepads and maps,

With charts, calculations and thousands of books,

And with worn-out expressions and desperate looks –

She looked at the sages, three hundred and more,

And thought, "I don't see why they've made such a chore

Out of something so simple, when everyone knows

The solution is really right under their nose..."

She said to the sages, "Now, this is the way –

You must start at once – yes, this very day!

Tell all of my subjects, old, young, big and small,

To come hear my question, right here in this hall,

And the one who can answer my question so clever

Will be my true friend forever and ever."

And the counselors all did stare

At the princess so wise and so fair:

"If you please, Your Highness," they said with a bow,

"What is your question? Oh, please let us know!"

"This is the question," she spoke again,

"That you must ask everyone, women and men –

Everyone coming from far and near –

This is the question I want them to hear:

What part of the body is the best,

Far more important than all of the rest,

For a friendship that will withstand every test?"

That is what the princess asked,

And the sages so clever, so learned and wise

Feared the princess would think

they were just clueless guys –

So each of them hastened to nod and agree:

"That's a very good question!"

(while thinking, "Let's see

Who can answer... It certainly cannot be me...")

They made signs and banners of canvas and wood

And hurried to hang them wherever they could:

On every wall and every tower,

In every inn and every bower,

On every tree and every door –

And in places where no sign had ever been before.

And on all the signs was the very same question:

What part of the body is the best,

Far more important than all of the rest,

For a friendship that will withstand every test?

If you can answer this question so clever,

The princess will be your true friend forever!

The following month, on the very first day,

People came from near and far away:

Little old ladies and men strong and tall,

Parents and teachers and children small –

And every last person, each of them all

Thought, "I am so clever; I am so bright;

I know the answer and I'll get it right!"

The princess stood at the castle gate,

And next to her a wise herald did wait

With a map of the castle, and in a loud voice

Directed the guests to the rooms of their choice –

Each room had the name of an organ or limb –

And they all watched the herald and listened to him.

"Now, all those who think the best part is the mouth:

Go down the first corridor, turn to the south,

And into the Red Room. Be quick! Don't delay!"

Then hundreds of people all headed that way,

With mouths that smile and mouths that frown

And mouths with corners up or down,

With mouths that whispered, mouths that yelled,

And even mouths with breath that smelled...

Then the princess came into the room and asked "Why

Do you think that the mouth is the truest reply?"

"I'll tell you, Your Highness," somebody said

(With a mouth that was almost too big for his head):

"The mouth can do anything friends need to do:

It can cheer and encourage – and laugh and joke, too!"

(And everyone whispered, "It's true!")

The princess just nodded and smiled, and said "Oh...

I'm not saying yes...

And I'm not saying no...

First I'll hear all the answers, and then I can say

Which answer has brought me a true friend today."

And the herald continued directing the throng

Of women and men who had waited so long:

"If you think that the very best part is the ear,

Your place is the Green Room; you'll find it right here

At the end of the corridor. Quick! Don't delay!"

Then hundreds of people all headed that way –

And some had ears like small pink shells,

And some had ears like big brown bells,

And some had earrings in their ears –

And some ears hadn't been washed for years...

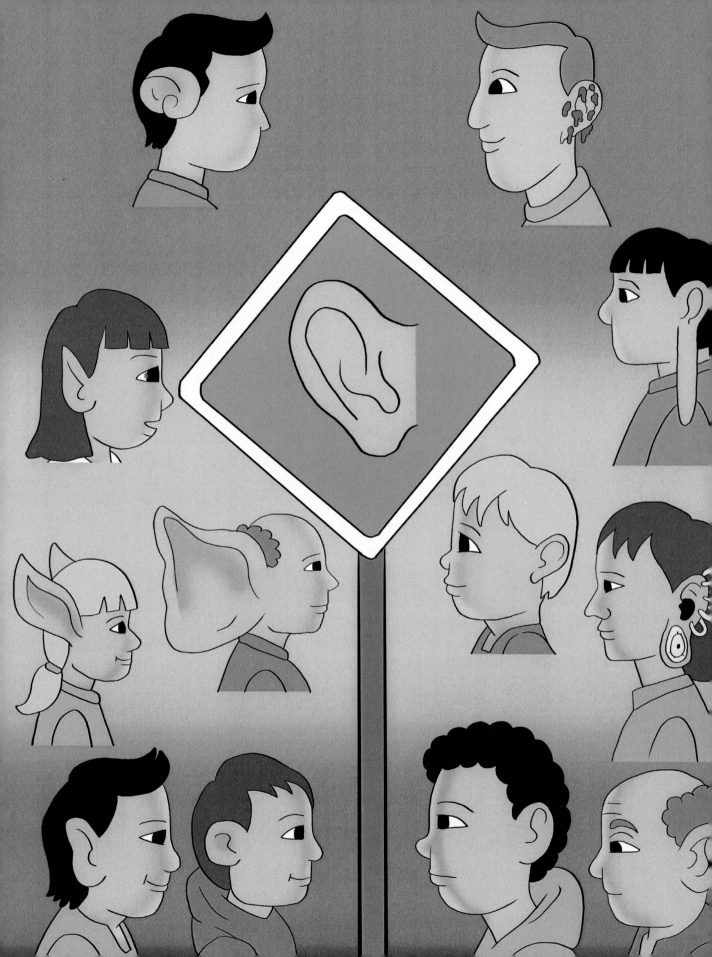

Then the princess came into the room and asked "How

Is the ear best for friendship? Please answer me now!"

"I'll tell you, Your Highness," someone replied

(With ears that were terribly long and wide):

"The ear can hear anything friends need to say;

It can listen forever, all night and all day!"

(And everyone cheered and said "Yay!")

The princess just nodded and smiled, and said "Oh...

I'm not saying yes...

And I'm not saying no...

First I'll hear all the answers, and then I can say

Which answer has brought me a true friend today."

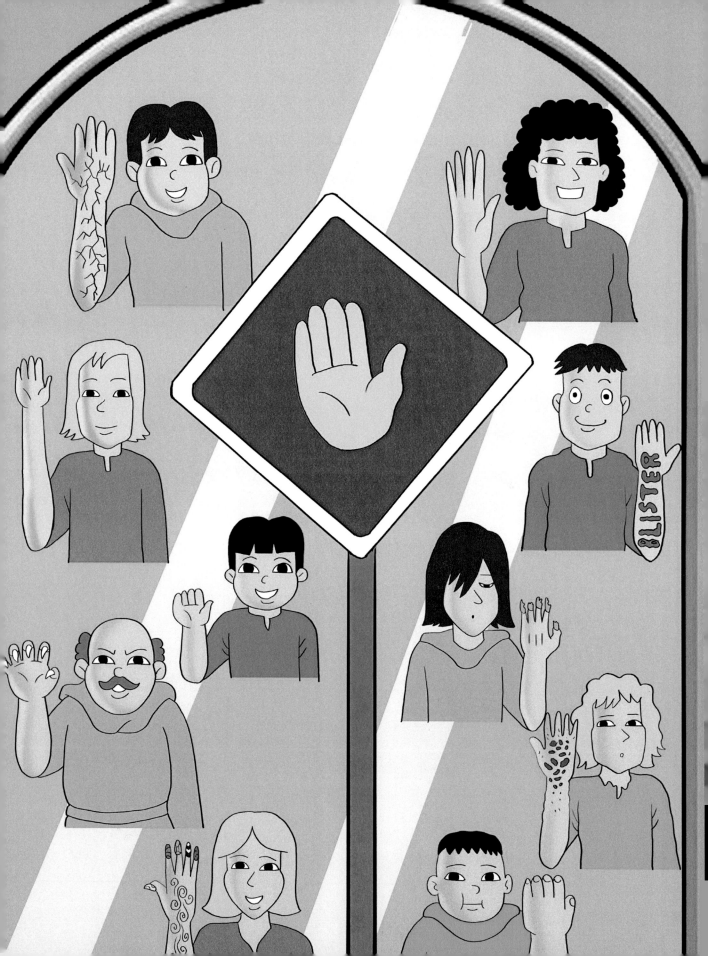

And the herald continued directing the crowd,

Waving the map and proclaiming out loud:

"If you think that the hand is the best part of all,

Take this corridor down to the Great Mirror Hall –

Wait for the princess there. Quick! Don't delay!"

Then hundreds of people all headed that way –

With tiny hands or great huge paws,

With polished nails or ragged claws,

With fingers long or short and stubby –

And some with hands all cracked and grubby...

Then the princess came into the room and asked

"Where Did you learn that the hand was the best?

Please share!"

"I'll tell you, Your Highness," someone spoke out

(Whose hand bore a gold ring that shone all about):

"The hand gives whatever friends need for a lift:

A comforting touch, or a push, or a gift!"

(And everyone smiled and nobody sniffed.)

The princess just nodded and smiled, and said "Oh...

I'm not saying yes...

And I'm not saying no...

First I'll hear all the answers, and then I can say

Which answer has brought me a true friend today."

And the herald continued directing the rest

Of the people: "If you think the heart is the best,

Go out to the garden and turn to the right;

At the end of the path is a door that is white –

It will lead to the White Room. Be quick! Don't delay!"

Then hundreds of people all headed that way –

And some had hearts that leapt with gladness,

And some had hearts bowed down by sadness,

Some hearts were bold and quite inspired –

And some were old and sick and tired...

Then the princess came into the room and asked

"Who Will say why the heart is the choice good and true?"

"I'll tell you Your Highness," somebody smiled

(With the virtuous heart of a good-natured child):

"The heart can help friends who are weary or sad:

It can love! Love heals troubles and makes the soul glad!"

(And everyone muttered, "Not bad!")

The princess just nodded and smiled, and said "Oh...

I'm not saying yes...

And I'm not saying no...

First I'll hear all the answers, and then I can say

Which answer has brought me a true friend today."

And the herald continued
to stand and to wait...
But now there was nobody
left at the gate!

They were all in the rooms,

for the princess to hear

Why the mouth,

or the hand,

or the heart,

or the ear

Was the best part.

The herald looked round

with dismay And thought

"I had better go home for the day" –

When a stranger sprang out

of the bush near the gate

And said "Do excuse me;

I hope I'm not late –

I've been going around

from one room to the next,

And I've heard all the answers –

and I'm quite perplexed:

All the answers were wise,

yes, and clever and sweet –

But none of the answers

was really complete:

There can't be one part

of the body that's best,

Far more important than all of the rest!

For a friendship to be strong

and true, every part –

The mouth and the ear

and the hand and the heart –

Must all work together,

with skill and with art.

Our ears help us listen, and point out the way

For our mouths to discover the right things to say;

Our hands can embrace, carry burdens and give,

And our hearts flow with love, understand and forgive –

So our friendships will last for as long as we live!"

And the princess smiled broadly; a light filled her eyes

And she spoke: "Oh, my friend, you are brilliant and wise!

Yes, this is the answer, the best there can be!

Come into the castle and stay here with me;

With our hearts and our hands and our mouths and our ears,

We'll be best friends forever, for many long years."

About the Author

Best seller author, Dr. Orly Katz (SimplyMeModel.com) is an expert on children and youth empowerment and the founder of the Simply Me Center for Leadership, Empowerment and Self Esteem.

She is the author of numerous books on Amazon under the "Simply Me" series:

(Surviving Junior High, Surviving Primary School and Busy Dizzy for ages 4-8).

Orly is also the creator and developer of the Simply Me-Digital Programs:

For teachers, parents and workshops facilitators:

"Empowering Adults to Empower Children".

Orly lives in Haifa, with her Husband and

three children.

www.SimplyMeAcademy.com

Thank you for taking the time to read:

"The Princess Who Wanted a Friend"

If you enjoyed it, please consider telling your

friends or posting a short review.

Word of mouth is an author's best friend

and much appreciated.

Thank you, again,

Dr. Orly Katz

www.SimplyMeAcademy.com

Other Books by Dr. Orly Katz:

Busy Dizzy- motivational
bedtime rhyming picture book for
children ages 4-8

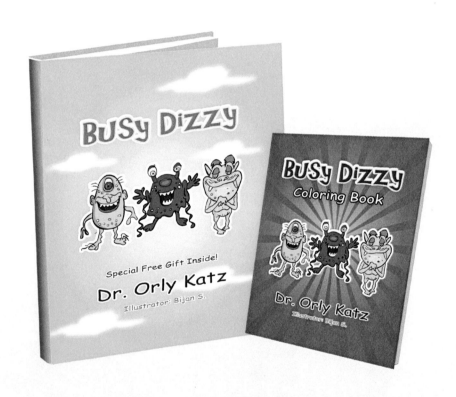

Other Books by Dr. Orly Katz:

Surviving Primary School

Other Books by Dr. Orly Katz:

Surviving Junior High

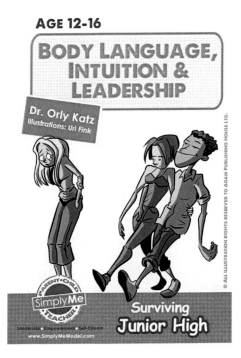

Made in the USA
San Bernardino, CA
14 September 2018